LILLY ™
LAUGHS

written and illustrated by
N.K. STOUFFER

Thurman House
Owings Mills, MD

Everyone laughed at little Lilly,

because she had a very big mouth.

Until...

one day Lilly began to laugh back.

[46] Mark Hugo Lopez, and D'Vera Cohn, Hispanic Poverty Rate Highest In New Supplemental Census Measure, http://www.pewhispanic.org/2011/11/08/hispanic-poverty-rate-highest-in-new-supplemental-census-measure/ (November 2011).

[47] Between Two Worlds: How Young Latinos Come of Age in America, http://www.pewhispanic.org/2009/12/11/between-two-worlds-how-young-latinos-come-of-age-in-america/ (December 2009).

[48] U.S. Hispanic Country of Origin Counts for Nation Top 30 Metropolitan Areas, http://www.pewhispanic.org/2011/05/26/us-hispanic-country-of-origin-counts-for-nation-top-30-metropolitan-areas/ (May 2011).

[49] The Mexican-American Boom: Births Overtake Immigration, http://www.pewhispanic.org/2011/07/14/the-mexican-american-boom-brbirths-overtake-immigration/ (July 2011).

[50] The Dark Side of Illegal Immigration, http://www.usillegalaliens.com/impacts_of_illegal_immigration_crime.html

[51] Illegal Immigration: The $113 Billion Dollar Drain on the American Taxpayer, http://www.illegalimmigrationstatistics.org/illegal-immigration-a-113-billion-a-year-drain-on-u-s-taxpayers/#more-331(September 2011).

[52] We express our gratitude to Numbers USA, and the Center for Immigration Studies, for its valuable information concerning historic immigration data which we extracted from its web site.

[53] John Bersente, and Mark Howard, Why the Federal Government Can't Recruit and Retain Hispanic-Americans, http://www.ere.net/2010/01/27/why-the-federal-government-can%E2%80%99t-recruit-and-retain-hispanic-americans/ (January 2011).

[54] John Patrick and Donald Ritchie, The Oxford Guide to the United States Government (USA, Oxford University Press), (2001).

Israel, Dioselina, Elia, Gabriel, Mrs. Audelia Corona. Maria G. Erazo, Elena and Alma. (Left to right back row, then front row)

PERSONAL NOTES

Observations concerning my own life and areas I want to change

_____

_____

_____

_____

_____

_____

_____

_____

_____

_____

_____

_____

_____

_____

_____

_____

In Search Of My Father

To place an order visit our web page

www.KairosTora.com

or

www.Amazon.com

She laughed,

and laughed,

and laughed!

She laughed when her brother

skinned his knee...

She laughed when a blind man

crossed the street...

She laughed when an old man

needed a cane to keep him on his feet....

She laughed at apples, and pears,

And yes, even meat...

She laughed so hard,

She couldn't speak...

She laughed,

and laughed,

and laughed

'til everyone cried!

She didn't laugh
'cause she didn't care...

She didn't laugh
'cause others were unlike her...

She didn't laugh
'cause she wasn't sad...

She didn't laugh
'cause she wasn't mad...

She laughed....

'cause she was laughed at,

and that's why Lilly laughed back!

It's never nice to laugh at others,

not for any reason, not ever!